REVENGE OF THE JUDOON

Terrance Dicks was born in East Ham, London. After university, he began work in the advertising industry before moving over to television as a writer. In 1968, he began working on *Doctor Who*. He has written more than sixty *Doctor Who* novels.

Revenge of the Judoon

Terrance Dicks

4 6 8 10 9 7 5

Published in 2008 by BBC Books, an imprint of Ebury Publishing.
Ebury Publishing is a division of the Random House Group Ltd.

Doctor Who is a BBC Wales production for BBC One
Executive Producers: Russell T Davies and Julie Gardner
Series Producer: Phil Collinson

The Random House Group Ltd Reg. No. 954009.
Addresses for companies within the Random House Group can be found
at www.randomhouse.co.uk.

A CIP catalogue record for this book is available from the British Library.

ISBN 978 1 84607 372 4

The Random House Group Limited supports the Forest Stewardship
Council (FSC), the leading international forest certification organisation.
All our titles that are printed on Greenpeace approved FSC certified
paper carry the FSC logo. Our paper procurement policy can be found
at www.rbooks.co.uk/environment

Series Consultant: Justin Richards
Project Editor: Steve Tribe
Cover design by Lee Binding © BBC 2008

Typeset in Stone Serif
Printed and bound in Great Britain by Cox & Wyman Ltd, Reading, Berkshire

Chapter One

A King
at Breakfast

Balmoral Castle lay bathed in autumn sunshine. The light shone on the white stone of the castle's ivy-covered walls. It sent golden shafts through the tall windows.

Captain Harry Carruthers, companion and aide to King Edward VII, marched along the red-carpeted corridors of the castle.

He glanced through the window. It was a beautiful day.

He sighed. On a day like this, the King would be sure to insist that he went outside and did something healthy. Not over-energetic himself, His Majesty liked to keep his guests busy.

Harry glanced up at the row of mounted stag-heads that lined the walls. There were so many that he wondered that there was a live stag left to shoot in all Scotland.

He climbed a staircase and moved along an

upper corridor – more red carpet, more stag-heads – and knocked on one of the doors.

A footman opened it, bowed respectfully, and led him through the richly furnished dressing room to the bedroom door on the far side. Throwing it open, the footman announced, 'Captain Carruthers, Your Majesty.' Then he bowed and withdrew.

Carruthers entered the bedroom. On the far side of the room, propped up on pillows in a four-poster bed, was the large figure of the King. His vast form, draped in a silk dressing gown, rose beneath the silk sheets.

His Majesty was breakfasting in bed. He chose from a range of dishes on a side table, served to him by a footman.

Carruthers bowed. 'Good morning, Your Majesty.'

Swallowing a mouthful of eggs and bacon, the King waved a hand. 'Morning, Harry. Splendid morning, eh?'

'Yes indeed, sir.'

The King passed his plate to the footman and wiped his moustache with a napkin. He sat up higher in bed, ready for business. 'Now then, what's the form?'

Carruthers produced a list of engagements for the days ahead and read it out loud. The next day there would be a visit to a new factory in Edinburgh, followed by a dinner with local officials the same evening. Then a return to London and the welcoming of a group of ambassadors, keen to present themselves to the new King.

It was a pretty heavy list, but the King accepted it cheerfully enough. One thing you could say for the old boy, thought Carruthers, for all his fondness for good food, fine wine and pretty ladies, his work never suffered. What's more he actually enjoyed royal occasions. Perhaps it was because he'd waited for so long for them. Now that he was King at last, he was making the most of it.

'But nothing today, eh?' said the King when Carruthers had finished.

'Nothing, Your Majesty. As you requested, today has been left completely free.'

'Excellent! Not often I get a day off! And that means it's a day off for you too.' The King considered. 'Tell you what you do. Go down to the gun room and borrow one of my sporting rifles. Time you broke your duck, three days and not a single stag. Go out and get yourself one. The country round here is full of them. Now isn't that a good idea?'

'A splendid idea, sir.'

Of course it was. After all, it was the King's idea – and they were all splendid.

'Off you go then,' said the King. 'Nothing like an early start. Take one of my Purdeys, why don't you? Damn fine guns, been using them for years, gave them my Royal Warrant back in 1868...'

An hour later, Harry Carruthers was striding through the woods that bordered Balmoral Castle. He'd changed his Guards uniform for comfortable tweeds, and he had a Purdey deer-rifle tucked under one arm.

He paused at the top of a little rise to gaze back at the castle, wondering if the King was up yet. Despite the sunshine, the morning air was crisp and chill.

'All very well, sending me out for a nice healthy tramp through the hills,' thought Carruthers. 'He'll spend the morning by the fire with a big cigar, a large brandy and *The Times*.'

He frowned, looking back at the castle. Here on the hillside it was still a fine autumn morning, but there seemed to be a rain cloud over the castle itself.

Freak Highland weather, thought Carruthers, as he turned to go on his way.

It was odd though, all the same.

Probably just a trick of the light.

Just for a moment he could have sworn it was raining *upwards*...

Chapter Two

A Golden
Age

Not far away, a blue police box faded into view on an empty Scottish hillside.

After a moment, the door opened. Two figures came out, a tall thin man and an attractive young girl.

The man drew in a deep breath of Highland air and gazed happily around him. 'Look at that,' cried the Doctor. 'Just look at that! Now, is that a view or is that a view?'

Martha Jones looked. It was certainly an attractive stretch of countryside. Not far away, there were pine woods leading down to the River Dee, the sun gleaming on its rushing waters. There were low wooded hills all around, gradually increasing to larger ones in the misty distance.

'Now that is a view!' said the Doctor, answering his own question. 'What do you say?'

'It's very nice,' said Martha.

'Very nice?' said the Doctor. 'Queen Victoria loved this bit of countryside. Called it her Highland paradise. She came to Balmoral Castle on a visit as a young girl, fell in love with it, bought the place, knocked the castle down, built a bigger one. That's the Royals for you – expense no object.' He shaded his eyes with his hand, peering into the distance. 'You can see the castle from here.' He frowned, turning slowly around, surveying the countryside. 'Well, you ought to be able to see it...'

'Perhaps they've moved it. Decided it would look nicer somewhere else.'

'No, no, they wouldn't do that,' said the Doctor. 'Would they?' He peered round again, shaking his head. 'Maybe they would. Can't understand why we can't see it... unless we're not where I think I am.' He licked his finger and held it up in the air as if that might give him a clue.

'Norway?' suggested Martha. 'China?'

'No,' said the Doctor. He inspected his finger. 'Might be about half a mile out. It can happen when you're crossing the universe.' He drew a deep breath. 'Just taste that Highland air. Can't mistake it!'

'Do I have to wear these clothes?' Martha

looked down at her long skirt and high-button boots. She adjusted the lapels of her heavy tweed jacket. She tugged at the collar of her high-necked white blouse.

'I searched the TARDIS wardrobe to find those clothes,' said the Doctor. 'Just what the well-bred young lady wears for a country stroll. Look at me, I'm not complaining.' He looked happily down at his hairy tweed suit. It was exactly the same cut as the suit he usually wore.

'All right for you, a suit's a suit,' grumbled Martha. 'Men's clothes never seem to change. Why are we bothering with these outfits?'

The Doctor sighed. 'What did you say to me in the TARDIS?'

'I said I wanted a bit of peace and quiet, a touch of gracious living. Somewhere without hostile aliens and nasty monsters.'

'Exactly. I promised you a visit to a golden age, a time of peace, prosperity and calm.' He threw his arms out wide, just missing Martha, and turned in a full circle on the spot. 'And here we are!'

'Where? No, I suppose I mean: when?'

'Very beginning of the twentieth century, early years of the reign of His Majesty King Edward the Seventh. The Boer War is just ending and the First World War is still years away. It's a golden age, but a more formal one, and that's why you've got to wear the clothes.'

'So what's the plan?'

'We soak up some healthy Highland air, then pop down to London to enjoy the high life. I might even get you presented at Court.'

'That sounds more like it.'

'Right,' said the Doctor. 'Come on!'

'Where?'

'To enjoy a nice bracing stroll through the countryside. We can find that missing castle while we're at it.'

Captain Harry Carruthers lay hidden behind a boulder on a nearby hillside, and wrestled with his conscience.

A few hundred yards away, across a shallow valley, was another little hill. On the crest of that hill stood a stag. And not just any old stag. A magnificent old twelve-pointer, well past its prime. A shootable stag, fair game for the hunter. It stood quite still, gazing into the distance.

Carruthers lay in the classic firing position, his rifle lined up on its target. His finger tightened on the trigger.

A touch more pressure and...

Harry Carruthers had a shameful secret. He didn't really like hunting. He was a fine shot. He had seen action in the Boer War and had shot quite a few Boer soldiers out of their saddles – but then, they'd been trying to shoot him.

But killing for sport, shooting at something that couldn't shoot back... Somehow he had no taste for it.

In this Edwardian age, such ideas in a young army officer would be regarded as very strange indeed. Hunting, shooting and fishing were a gentleman's natural pursuits.

So Harry Carruthers kept his secret and played along, missing as often as he decently could. Now he had a problem. He'd been ordered to shoot a stag by the King himself. The perfect stag had appeared. And orders were orders. He drew a deep breath and steadied his aim...

'My heart's in the Highlands, my heart is not here,' sang the Doctor, in a surprisingly good Scots accent. 'My heart's in the Highlands a-hunting the deer.'

'You're not the only one,' said Martha. She pointed.

Clearly visible on a hillside just ahead, a young man was training his rifle on a noble stag, which stood on the crest of a nearby hill.

They saw the young man take aim.

'Oi!' shouted Martha.

The stag ran. The young man fired – and missed.

As the stag vanished over the other side of the hill, the young man rose. He came towards them, cradling the rifle in the crook of one arm.

'You made me miss my shot,' said the young man mildly. He didn't seem very annoyed.

'Yeah, well, I don't approve of blood sports,' said Martha firmly.

The young man was slim and fair, and slight in build. He wasn't much taller than she was herself. But he was, Martha suddenly realised, extremely handsome.

He gave her a charming smile. 'Not sure I approve of blood sports myself. But he was a very old stag, you know. He'll die soon anyway, perhaps in pain.'

'So you were doing him a favour?' Martha's tone made it very clear she didn't believe it.

'Well...'

'No point worrying about it now,' said the Doctor quickly. 'Allow me to introduce Miss Martha Jones, my ward. Where she comes from they have no tradition of stag hunting. There aren't any stags. Tigers, yes, very touchy tigers, they hate being hunted...'

The young man bowed. 'An honour to meet

you, Miss Jones. To be honest, I'm not too bothered about missing the stag myself. But I'm afraid you've got me in trouble with my employer.'

Martha gave him a puzzled look. 'How come?'

'He sent me out this morning with orders to shoot a stag.'

Martha snorted. 'Who does your boss think he is, giving orders like that? King of England?'

The young man looked at her and smiled. 'Actually, he does. And, as a matter of fact, he is!'

Martha stared at him. 'What are you on about? Are you saying you work for the King?'

'I am – and I do. What's more, I think it's your duty to explain to His Majesty that you made me miss my shot. My life may depend on it!'

Martha looked horrified. 'You're not serious? Doctor, he's not serious is he?'

'Very serious matter, disobeying the King,' said the Doctor. 'Could mean the Tower!'

'You're joking.'

Harry Carruthers grinned. 'He's joking. Don't worry. The most the old boy will do is pull my leg about being a rotten shot.'

The Doctor smiled. 'I take it you're based at Balmoral?'

Carruthers bowed. 'Captain Harry Carruthers, aide to His Majesty King Edward the Seventh.'

'Doctor John Smith.'

Carruthers turned to Martha. 'Tell you what, why don't you come back to Balmoral for lunch? I'll introduce you to his Majesty. He loves meeting new people – especially if they're attractive and female.' He gave Martha an admiring look.

'You'd better watch out Martha,' said the Doctor. 'One of His Majesty's popular nicknames is "Edward the Caresser".'

Harry Carruthers laughed. 'Your ward will be safe enough, sir. At the moment Lillie Langtry and Mrs Keppel are keeping him fully occupied.' He turned to Martha. 'Will you accept?'

'Oh, I don't know,' said the Doctor. 'Busy schedule, tour of the Highlands, trip to London. We wouldn't want to impose.'

But Martha felt differently. 'Oh come on, Doctor,' she said. 'How often do you get the chance to have lunch with a king?'

After a few more polite protests, they accepted the invitation.

'Right, come along then,' said Carruthers. 'Allow me to lead the way.'

He set off down the path.

As they followed, the Doctor whispered,

'Quite often, actually.'

'Quite often what?' asked Martha.

'Quite often I've lunched with a king. Henry the Eighth always put on a good spread... James the First was surprisingly mean. And as for Alfred the Great – the venison stew was all right, but the cakes were terrible...'

'Sssh!' said Martha.

'Not much further,' said Carruthers over his shoulder. 'There's a good view of the castle when we get to the top of this next hill.'

He strode ahead, reached the top of the hill – and froze.

'No!' he gasped.

The Doctor and Martha hurried to join him.

Below them there should have been the splendid sight of Balmoral Castle.

But there wasn't.

Instead, there was a vast, oddly shaped area of bare earth, a shallow crater, surrounded by gardens, fountains and paths.

The Doctor and Martha looked at each other. Then, both speaking at once, they said one word.

'*Judoon!*'

Chapter Three

Hunt for
a Castle

Harry Carruthers gave them a stunned stare. 'What?'

Martha looked at the Doctor. 'Judoon,' she said again. 'It's got to be, hasn't it, Doctor?'

'The technique does seem familiar,' agreed the Doctor. 'The Judoon, or a gang of very eager workmen with a very, very, *very* large crane.'

The Doctor and Martha had come across the Judoon before. In fact, it was how they'd met. The hospital where Martha had been a medical student had been whisked away to the moon by the Judoon. They had taken Martha and the Doctor with it.

In the dangerous events that followed, Martha had learned that the high-tech Judoon were a sort of police force for hire. They'd hijacked the hospital in their hunt for a murderous shape-changing Plasmavore, a kind of space vampire.

In the end, like the Canadian Mounties, the Judoon had got their man – or rather old woman. The Plasmavore had been disguised as an elderly female patient.

In the process, they'd risked the lives of the Doctor, Martha and a whole hospital full of doctors, nurses and patients. The Judoon were ruthlessly single-minded in their pursuit of what they saw as justice.

The Doctor was fishing a slender torch-like device out of his pocket. He adjusted its controls then waved it towards the gaping crater. The device buzzed and clicked.

'Plasma coil traces,' said the Doctor. 'It's the Judoon all right.'

He switched off the device and put it away.

Harry Carruthers, slowly getting over the shock, looked from one to the other of them. 'Look, who are you? What's going on? And who the devil are these *Judoon*?'

The Doctor sighed. Explaining was always the difficult bit. 'I'm the Doctor and this is Martha. At the moment, I've no idea what's going on. And the Judoon...' He paused. 'Let's just say they're an alien race with the ability to cause what's happened here.'

Carruthers shook his head. 'But it's impossible...'

The Doctor waved towards the crater below. 'But it's happened,' he said gently. 'You don't have to believe me, but you must believe your own eyes.'

Carruthers was struggling to understand. 'You said an alien race. You mean from outer space? Like in the books by that chap Wells? *War of the Worlds* and all that?'

'Very like,' agreed the Doctor. 'Except a Judoon is more like a giant rhino than a giant octopus.'

'But that's just fantasy,' said Carruthers. 'Just imagination.'

'Oh, come on,' snapped the Doctor. 'There are thousands of planets in the galaxy and millions of galaxies. Do you really imagine your little Earth is the only one to support intelligent life forms?' Turning away, he studied the crater. 'To shift something that size, they'd have needed some kind of plasma beacon to focus the energy. Somehow they must have smuggled one inside the castle.' He turned back to Carruthers. 'Think carefully. Did you see any kind of advanced alien device inside the castle?'

'I don't think so... What would it look like? Something very big?'

'Doesn't have to be. A glass sphere probably, about the size of a cricket ball. There might be some kind of spinning energy vortex inside, like a sort of whirlwind.'

Carruthers looked stunned. 'I can tell you exactly where it was, Doctor. It was in my luggage. I took it into the castle.' He looked at the crater where the castle had once stood. He grabbed the Doctor's arm and said wildly, 'Don't you see? *I'm* responsible! I'm responsible for this!'

Gently the Doctor freed his arm. 'Captain Carruthers, you're not responsible for this – the Judoon are. The Judoon and whoever's behind them.'

'What do you mean, behind them?' asked Martha.

'The Judoon don't act alone,' said the Doctor. 'Somebody's employed them, hired them to do this.'

'But why?'

'That's one of the things we've got to find out,' said the Doctor.

'You?' Carruthers said in disbelief.

'Oh yes,' the Doctor told him.

'You bet,' Martha added.

'Who else is qualified?' the Doctor asked. 'Anyway, I resent people mucking about with old buildings. And we have a more selfish reason...'

'Well?' said Carruthers.

'What's happened here puts Martha's entire future in danger – her friends and family too.'

'How so?'

'Huge interference with the timeline,' said the Doctor. 'No King Edward the Seventh means no George the Fifth, so no George the Sixth.'

Carruthers began to splutter, but the Doctor carried on regardless.

'No Elizabeth the Second, God bless her, and no King Charles the Third and Queen Camilla, no King William the Fifth – no, you haven't got there yet, have you? Anyway you see what I mean.'

'Not exactly, no,' Martha said. 'And the Royals affect me and my family because...?'

'*Everyone's* life will be disrupted,' said the Doctor. 'All human history changed. This might only be the start of it. Imagine – castles going missing all over Britain. Anything could happen. Or not happen. Your mum might never meet your dad and you'd never be born. We've got to sort this out.'

'Nothing to do with a certain person being completely unable to mind his own business, I suppose?'

'Certainly not,' said the Doctor. 'A Time Lord's got to do what a Time Lord's got to do.' He nudged her shoulder gently. 'And it'll be fun. I mean, aren't you curious – just a tiny bit?'

Harry Carruthers was staring wildly at them. 'What the devil are you two talking about? We've got to do something.'

'Oh yes,' said the Doctor. 'And you can help us.'

'I can? How?'

'You say *you* brought the plasma beacon to the castle. The glass sphere with the spinning vortex. You didn't just find it lying in the gutter, did you? So, tell us, where did you get it? Who gave it to you?'

'My doctor,' said Carruthers. 'Good grief, another doctor. This business is full of doctors. Well actually, he's not my doctor any longer. Used to be our family doctor, but he gave up medicine years ago. He's a writer now.'

'Name?' asked the Doctor patiently.

'Arthur. Arthur Conan Doyle.'

'The Sherlock Holmes man?' Martha said.

'That's right.'

'Arthur Conan Doyle?' the Doctor said. 'How did Arthur Conan Doyle come to give you the device? Why did he give you the device? I mean, where did he get the device?'

Carruthers shrugged. 'He turned up at my rooms the night before I came up to Balmoral.

20

Seemed very worried. I was surprised to see him. We'd met once or twice since he gave up medicine, but we weren't close.'

'Go on.' The Doctor waggled his fingers, teasing out the man's story.

'He produced this glass sphere with a kind of spinning light inside. Said it was a scientific breakthrough, a possible energy source of great power. Begged me to take it to Balmoral, and show it to the King. He wanted me to persuade the King to pass it on to the top scientific fellows in the Royal Society. Said he was writing a report explaining everything, but he was desperate to get the device into safe hands.'

'So you agreed?'

'Well not at first. But he went on and on, seemed so frantic. And, well, the thing looked harmless enough. Sort of a fancy crystal ball. I thought it might amuse His Majesty. So I gave in and took it.'

'What happened then?'

'He swore me to secrecy before he left.'

'Did he say where he'd got this crystal ball thing?' asked Martha.

'Not a word. To tell the truth I wasn't really interested enough to ask. Seemed like a parlour trick – as I said, an amusement. I chucked it into my bag and forgot about it.'

'Weren't you surprised by all this? asked Martha.

'Very much so.'

'Well, I'm not,' said the Doctor. 'I met him once. On the outside, he's a big serious chap with a big serious moustache. Typical Victorian gent. But there's a side of him that loves his ghosts and goblins and fairies.'

'And aliens?' suggested Martha.

'Could be,' said the Doctor. 'He'd be a sucker for a friendly alien with a good story.'

'So what do we do now?' Martha asked.

'Oh, I think that's pretty obvious.'

'It is?'

'Captain Carruthers, I need your help.'

'Of course, anything I can do,' said Carruthers.

'Take Martha back to London. Find Conan Doyle and make him tell you where he got the glass sphere. Then come and tell me what he says.'

'And what will you be doing?' asked Martha.

'I've got a missing castle to track down,' the Doctor told her.

'And then?'

'I'll get inside the castle, do the tour. Maybe pop into the gift shop and get the T-shirt. And find out just what's going on.'

'Now wait a minute,' said Martha. 'I'm coming with you. Captain Carruthers can chase Conan Doyle on his own.'

'Martha,' said the Doctor. 'I need your help too. I can't be in two places at once. The information you're going after is vital. And you're the only one who can get it to me.'

Martha knew what he meant. The Doctor had soniced her mobile phone so it had a near-endless battery life and an amazing range.

'You're not just sending me out of danger?' she asked suspiciously.

'I'm just worried I'm sending you *into* danger,' said the Doctor. 'At least I know what I'll be facing. You don't!'

Chapter Four

The Sherlock Holmes Man

Captain Carruthers was recovering from his shock. Still confused, he was determined to get a grip on the situation.

'Hadn't we better give the alarm about all this?' He waved at the gaping crater.

'Certainly not,' said the Doctor. 'For one thing, there's no need. Even in the remote Highlands of Scotland, someone's going to notice a missing castle after a while. But with any luck, it may not happen for a bit. For the moment, the less fuss the better.'

'If you say so, Doctor,' said Carruthers. 'Well, if we're going to go back to London, we'd better get moving. There's a train at—'

'Take far too long,' said the Doctor.

'What then?'

'I'll give you a lift,' said the Doctor. 'Get you there much quicker.'

'Quicker than a train?'

'Much quicker,' said Martha.

'I say, you haven't got one of these new-fangled flying machines? Like those Wright Brothers in America? There's a French fellow called Bleriot swears he's going to fly the channel. Pilot are you, Doctor?'

'After a fashion,' said the Doctor. 'Pioneer, certainly. Come on, time we got moving.'

As they set off back down the hill, Martha smiled to herself. Captain Harry Carruthers was in for another shock.

In fact, Carruthers accepted the journey back to London in a police box that hadn't been invented yet quite calmly. It was as if his powers of astonishment were all used up.

Even the fact that the TARDIS was bigger on the inside than the outside hadn't thrown him too much. He looked round the complex control room and said drily, 'Most impressive.'

The Doctor busied himself setting controls at the central console for quite some time.

'Sorry it's taking so long,' he said to them after a while. 'Believe it or not, these short trips are trickier than long ones. Pluto would be easier than Piccadilly. There's the time factor too – don't want to arrive before we set off.' He stared into space. Then he shook his head. 'No, definitely not.'

At last, the Doctor was happy, and the central column began its rise and fall.

A few minutes later, the TARDIS was standing on the corner of a quiet side street just by Piccadilly Circus.

The Doctor opened the doors, and Martha peered out. She always felt a thrill of excitement at finding out where they were.

Sure enough, there were the familiar London streets, jammed not with cars but with crowded horse-drawn buses and hansom cabs. No tube station – that wouldn't open until 1906, in a few more years – and no neon signs. But there was Eros. It was Piccadilly Circus all right.

'Off you go then,' said the Doctor. 'Good luck. Don't forget, Martha, get in touch as soon as you can.'

They left the TARDIS and watched as it faded away. It had come and gone so quickly that nobody seemed to notice. Or if they did, they didn't believe their eyes.

Carruthers raised his hand and hailed a hansom cab. 'Mount Street please, driver!'

'Where are we going?' asked Martha.

'My rooms.'

'Why?'

'My dear girl, I can't go parading about Town in country tweeds.'

Despite Martha's protests, Carruthers would not be swayed. Then, when they reached his rooms, he tried to make Martha wait outside.

'My man's on holiday, and you can't possibly be alone with me in my rooms. What about your reputation?'

'Yeah, well we're not likely to meet anyone who knows me.'

Martha waited in Carruthers' little sitting room until he appeared in a dark suit, complete with hat, stick and gloves.

'Very nice,' said Martha. 'Now can we go and find your friend Doyle? It is urgent, you know.'

'We'll try the Grand in Northumberland Avenue first. He nearly always stays there.'

The horse-drawn hansom cab drew up outside the entrance of a large hotel.

'There you are, sir,' called the driver. 'Grand Hotel.'

Harry Carruthers got out and helped Martha to climb down. He paid the driver, who touched his hat, cracked his whip and drove away.

Carruthers turned to Martha. 'As I said, he usually stays here when he's in London. But if not, there are one or two others we could try.'

He took her inside.

They were in luck, however – Doyle *was* staying at the hotel. Carruthers told them at the reception desk that he was an old friend of Doyle's, here on urgent business. He insisted on being shown up to his room.

At the top of a short staircase they were shown through the door of a first-floor suite.

They entered a smartly furnished sitting room. At the same moment, a big man with a large moustache came in through the bedroom doors.

He held out his hand. 'Harry! I thought you were still at Balmoral.'

'I was, until a very short time ago. Allow me to introduce my friend Miss Jones, a visitor from...' He broke off, realising he had no idea where Martha was actually from. 'Er, Miss Jones, Sir Arthur Conan Doyle – famous creator of Sherlock Holmes.'

Sir Arthur frowned.

'More importantly, an eminent doctor and a famous historical novelist,' added Carruthers quickly.

Sir Arthur beamed and bowed. 'An honour, Miss Jones. Please, be seated.'

Doyle sat in a huge leather armchair, Martha and Carruthers on a velvet sofa.

'Congratulations on the knighthood, Sir Arthur,' said Carruthers. 'A Royal nod, you might say.'

'What do you mean?'

'They say His Majesty's a great Sherlock Holmes fan, wants more stories from you.'

'The honour had nothing to do with Holmes,' protested Doyle. 'I've killed the fellow off, you know. He was distracting attention from my work as a historical novelist. The knighthood was for writing *The War in South Africa: Its Causes and Conduct*. And of course for my medical work.' He turned to Martha. 'Tried to get into the fighting but they wouldn't have me! So I went out as a doctor.'

Martha felt it was time to get down to business. 'We've come to see you on a very urgent matter, Sir Arthur. We need your help.'

'Of course, my dear. Anything I can do.'

'You remember visiting me in my rooms, Arthur, just before I set off for Balmoral?' asked Carruthers. 'You gave me a device – a crystal sphere with a spinning light inside.'

Doyle looked at Martha. 'This is a very private matter, Captain Carruthers.'

'Miss Jones has my full confidence,' said Carruthers. He had a sudden idea. 'Miss Jones is assistant to a very noted scientist – a certain

29

Doctor Smith, who is very interested in your device.'

Carruthers turned to Martha for support.

'The Doctor thinks the device has great potential as an energy source,' she said solemnly. 'But he wants to know more about it – like where you got it from.'

'That's right,' said Carruthers. 'Who gave it to you? Where did it come from?'

Doyle looked worried, and his big frame shifted uneasily. 'I am not at liberty to say. I was told—'

'Unless you confide in us, the matter can go no further,' said Carruthers sternly. 'The benefits of the device will be lost to humanity.'

Doyle still looked doubtful.

'Just tell us who gave it to you,' urged Martha. 'That's all. Then we can go and ask them about it. It's up to them what they tell us then. Please, Sir Arthur. You must tell us!'

Chapter Five

The Cosmic Peacemakers

There was a moment's pause, then Conan Doyle said, 'Very well.'

He rose and strode up and down on the thick Turkish carpet.

'On my return from South Africa, I was invited to join a highly secret scientific society – the Cosmic Peacemakers. I'd heard rumours about them for some time. Their work lies on the extreme frontiers of science.' He paused. 'They concern themselves with the spiritual side of science, as well as the purely mechanical. They believe that it is possible to contact other planes, other worlds.'

'Just the sort of thing the Doctor said Doyle would be a sucker for,' thought Martha. Out loud she said, 'Sounds fascinating. Go on.'

'After I'd attended several of their meetings, they produced this device. They said it came from beyond this Earth. I was urged to make it known to the highest authorities. They suggested the King himself.'

'Where are these people based?' asked Carruthers.

Again Doyle hesitated.

'Please,' said Martha. 'All we need is an address.'

'They have a laboratory,' said Doyle. 'It is in Black Dog Lane, an alley behind the wharves to the east of London Bridge. It's not easy to find.'

'How do we get there?' asked Carruthers.

'You reach it by a steep flight of steps between a gin palace and an old clothes shop. It's a sordid area, but it gives them the privacy they need.'

'I bet,' murmured Martha.

'Thank you,' said Carruthers.

Outside the hotel, Carruthers asked, 'What now?'

Martha had a strange hollow feeling. Was it fear? Was a disaster coming? She looked up at Carruthers.

'What's the matter, Miss Jones?'

'I just realised – I never got that royal lunch you promised me. I never got any lunch at all. I'm starving!'

Carruthers looked guilty. 'My dear young lady,' he said. 'Don't worry, I know the very place.'

He waved his stick, and a passing hansom cab stopped beside them. 'Golden Rose Restaurant, please, cabbie.'

Half an hour later, they were sitting in a quiet booth in a little Soho restaurant. There were flowers and a lighted candle at their table. The whole place had a warm and intimate feel. There was even a gypsy violinist.

Soon Martha and Carruthers were tucking into an excellent meal of steak and chips. Carruthers washed it down with a bottle of wine.

'You think we should visit this laboratory?' Carruthers asked as they ate.

'What do you think?' Martha said. 'No point in stopping now that we're getting somewhere.'

'Of course,' said Carruthers. 'But shouldn't you speak to the Doctor first?'

'And tell him what? A weird name and a dodgy address? We've got nothing worth telling him – yet.'

'So what do you suggest?

'A visit to Black Dog Lane, and the laboratory of the Cosmic Peacemakers.'

Carruthers was looking worried. 'That could

be dangerous. I don't think the Doctor would approve.'

'Well, he's not here, is he?' said Martha cheerfully. 'Anyway, he loves danger – you ask him.' She frowned. 'And I'm sure he's in it up to his neck!'

The Doctor was staring at the scanner screen in the TARDIS control room. It was showing a view of the planet Earth as seen from space. This was natural enough, since the TARDIS was in a parking orbit around the planet.

The Doctor needed to trace the plasma coil currents to their final destination. He had spent a lot of time estimating their path. Now he was about to see if he was correct.

Flexing long thin fingers, he reached out and pressed the final control.

The image on the screen grew larger and larger until it showed what looked like a blank space with an energy pulse at its centre.

The Doctor rubbed his hands together. 'Still haven't lost my touch. Eat your heart out, Google Earth!'

He studied the data flowing across the bottom of the screen.

'There you go – slap bang in the middle of the Empty Quarter. Two hundred and fifty thousand square miles of Arabian desert. The most deserted place on Earth. But not any more, it seems.'

He touched more controls and the screen disappeared. The Doctor turned back to the console.

'Here we go!' He paused. 'I wonder why Martha's taking so long to get in touch...'

'Here you are, lady and gent,' said the cab driver. 'Corner of Black Dog Lane. You're on foot from now on. Street's too narrow to take the cab down, even if I wanted to, which I don't. And don't you ask me to wait, because I'm not going to, not round here.'

Carruthers and Martha got out. Carruthers paid the driver, and the cab rattled away.

Black Dog Lane – it was more of an alley really – lived up to the promise of its name. It was dark, dank, dirty, very smelly and probably visited by lots of dogs. The scents of the nearby river – muddy water, tar, warehouses full of tea and coal and spices – mixed with far more unpleasant smells from the open sewer that ran down the middle of the street.

The lane itself ran between tall, rickety buildings that seemed to lean forward as if to crush it.

'Yuk!' said Martha, summing it all up.

'Charming spot,' murmured Carruthers. 'Want to turn back?'

'Certainly not. Come on!'

They set off down the alley, avoiding the worst of the puddles and trying not to step in anything too unpleasant.

The first of their landmarks, the gin palace, was easy to find. Its lights blazed halfway down the gloomy alley. Martha and Carruthers could hear loud voices and louder music.

As they drew nearer, they saw a number of huddled bodies lying on the pavement nearby.

They stopped, not wanting to get too close. Martha was horrified but Carruthers seemed to take it all for granted.

'Typical gin mill, drunk for tuppence, dead drunk for sixpence.'

Martha looked at the shop they'd stopped outside. Its grimy windows held piles of old clothes, so shabby it seemed impossible anyone would buy them.

'And here's the old clothes shop,' she said. 'So the steps should be just a little further on.'

And so they were. They led steeply down to a little area. In the wall on the left, Martha could just make out a heavy door with a small light burning above it.

Carruthers led the way down the steps, and they paused outside the door. There was no bell and no knocker, so Carruthers hammered loudly on the door with his fist. But nothing happened.

Martha took off her heavy walking shoe and used that, banging away at the door as hard as she could.

This did get a result. A hatch opened in the upper part of the door and a skull-like face looked out. A cold, creaking voice said, 'Go away, you drunken fools, or it'll be the worse for you.'

'We're here on important business,' shouted Martha. 'We come from Sir Arthur Conan Doyle.'

'Official government business,' shouted Carruthers. 'Open in the name of the King!'

The hatch slammed shut, and Martha thought that was it.

But, a few moments later, the door creaked open, and they both stared in astonishment.

A white-haired, white-robed figure with a thin handsome face stood just inside the doorway, bathed in a golden glow. It spoke in a voice of mellow sweetness.

'Enter, my children. Welcome to the home of the Cosmic Peacemakers.'

The figure stepped back, beckoning Martha and Carruthers inside.

They went through into the golden glow. The heavy door slammed shut behind them.

Chapter Six

The Empty
Quarter

For a brief moment, the silence of the desert was disturbed by a strange wheezing, groaning sound. A blue police box materialised on top of a sand dune.

The Doctor came out, reeling a little in the fierce heat. Feeling that heavy tweeds wouldn't do for the desert, he'd changed back into one of his usual pinstripe suits. But even in that he was far too hot.

He considered going back inside for shorts and decided he couldn't be bothered. He looked at the scene around him.

All around there was sand, mile upon mile of it. Weirdly shaped dunes with oddly patterned sides, like the one he was now standing on. Flat rolling areas with complex patterns traced in the sand. Nothing but sand – in every direction but one.

There, directly in front of him, at the bottom of a huge shallow bowl in the desert, was an enormous building. Or rather, several buildings, linked by lower wings. There was a massive square tower on one corner and a smaller round one close by.

'Balmoral Castle,' murmured the Doctor. 'Oh, you are such an excellent example of over-the-top Victorian Gothic! So what on Earth are you doing here?'

In the distance, just beyond the castle, stood a cluster of three giant metal columns. They were as tall as tower blocks, and stood on stubby legs which extended outwards from the base of the column. They were Judoon spaceships.

'And why *here*?' he wondered.

Maybe the Judoon, with their usual directness, had just picked out the biggest blank space on the planet and plonked down their spaceships and their stolen castle in the middle of it.

The Doctor noticed that the castle was covered with an almost invisible transparent dome. There was a kind of shimmering blur, quite distinct from the desert heat haze.

With a sudden crack, a bullet whizzed past his head. The Doctor dropped flat in the sand.

Slowly, he raised his head. White-robed horsemen were thundering down the sides of

40

the bowl. They were shouting and screaming and firing their rifles in the air – desert raiders, carrying out their usual noisy charge to terrify their enemies. Coming across the castle in the desert must have seemed a great opportunity for a spot of looting.

This time, the Doctor suspected, they were out of luck.

The leading horseman charged towards the castle and bounced back, repelled by an invisible wall. The shock of the impact sent him flying from his horse. The horse itself staggered back and collapsed in the sand.

More and more attackers rode up, only to suffer the same fate. Soon the area in front of the castle was a tangle of fallen men and rearing horses. Shouts and screams and curses floated up as the angry horsemen struggled to regain their mounts and their places in the saddle.

They managed it at last, and regrouped. They milled about for a while, with much swearing and shouting and shooting. But their bullets pinged off the force field round the castle. Finally, frustrated and angry, they disappeared into the desert, in search, no doubt, of easier prey.

The Doctor waited until the last hoof beats had died away, then got up and made his way down the side of the dune towards the castle. He had to find some way to get inside. Something better than charging on horseback, screaming and firing a rifle.

'Still, it did look pretty,' he thought as he trudged across the sand. 'A good old-fashioned cavalry charge. Straight out of *Lawrence of Arabia* – or do I mean *Carry On Up the Khyber*? Possibly *Spamalot...*'

Martha and Carruthers were waiting for the Cosmic Peacemaker who had greeted them to return. He had introduced himself as Professor Challoner, then excused himself shortly after the beginning of their meeting.

To Martha it almost felt like she had moved from the past, the hansom cabs and gin places of Edwardian London, to the future. The room they sat in was furnished all in white. The furniture was spare and simple, and the glass walls glowed with an inner light.

Professor Challoner came back into the room, his thin face full of concern. Three white-robed figures followed him, all tall and thin and saintly looking.

'These are my colleagues. They are very anxious to hear what you have to say. Forgive the slight delay. I had something very important to attend to. Now, the device caused a disaster, you say? I was assured that it was harmless. Otherwise, of course, I should never have given it to our friend Doyle. Please, tell me what happened.'

Carruthers had carefully avoided any mention of the missing Balmoral Castle, and wasn't quite sure what to say. He looked hopefully at Martha.

'We're not quite sure,' said Martha. 'The reports from Scotland are still a bit confused, and no one seems to know quite what's going on. What we need to know, Professor, is what the device is. What's it for? And more importantly, where did you get it?'

Challoner sighed. 'I only wish I could be more helpful. The purpose, as I understand it, is to act as some kind of energy source. Huge power stored in a very small space.'

'And where does it come from? Was it developed here, in these laboratories?' asked Carruthers.

'No. It came from abroad. It was invented, or discovered, by one of our foreign colleagues. The device came from a monastery in Tibet – a great source of ancient wisdom.'

'Can you contact these colleagues?' asked Martha. 'Get them to tell us what we need to know.'

'Naturally, I shall do so immediately,' said Professor Challoner. 'However, it may take some little while. It is difficult to reach such a remote part of the world...'

Martha nodded. 'I understand. Please do what you can. We mustn't take up any more of your time.'

They rose and Professor Challoner showed them to the door.

Martha paused. 'I wonder if we could take a look round your laboratories before we go?'

Challoner shook his head sadly. 'Quite out of the question, I fear. Our work here is extremely advanced. It would be baffling, and possibly dangerous. If you will come this way?'

Minutes later, they were again climbing the dirty steps that led back up to Black Dog Lane.

'What do you make of that?' asked Carruthers as they reached the alley.

'He was playing for time,' said Martha. 'Monastery in Tibet, my foot.'

'Well, we didn't learn much, did we?'

'Oh, I don't know,' said Martha. 'As the Doctor says, know your enemy. At least we got a look at him. And at his HQ. That room we sat in...'

'What about it?'

'Did you ever see lighting like that before?'

'Well, no. But I'm not an expert at what

is possible with the new forms of electric lighting.'

'That room doesn't belong in this time. And there was something else...'

'What?'

'You remember that face that appeared in the hatch and tried to to send us away?'

Carruthers shuddered. 'Regular death's head.'

'Then the door opened and there was saintly old Challoner.'

'Well, it couldn't have been the same man,' said Carruthers. 'They must have an ugly doorman who went to get him. Doorman left, Challoner appeared.'

Martha shook her head. 'There wasn't time.'

'But what does that mean?'

Martha shrugged. 'I don't know. But it might mean that Challoner can change his shape. Hideous to saintly in a second!'

They left Black Dog Lane and walked towards the place where they'd got out of the cab.

'What now?' asked Carruthers. 'Are you going to get in touch with the Doctor?'

'Not yet. Let's go back and see your friend Sir Arthur. He told us he spent some time with this Cosmic Peacemaker lot. He must have learned something about them, and I don't think he was telling us everything he knows.'

They had to walk for some time before they reached an area where they could find another cab. When one appeared at last, Carruthers hailed it.

'Grand Hotel, cabbie.'

They got out of the cab, and Carruthers paid off the driver. As they turned to enter the hotel, they saw Sir Arthur Conan Doyle himself coming out.

'Arthur!' called Carruthers. 'Just the man we need! Glad we caught you.'

Conan Doyle looked at him in amazement. 'Harry? I thought you were still in Scotland! And who's your charming young friend?'

Carruthers stared. 'You know I'm not in Scotland. We came to see you just over an hour ago.'

'Nonsense, dear boy,' said Conan Doyle. 'Don't be silly, now. You know I haven't seen you for nearly a month.'

Chapter Seven

The
Judoon

Harry Carruthers stared at Conan Doyle in utter astonishment. 'Steady on, Arthur old chap. I introduced you to Miss Jones.'

'When? I'm sure I'd remember.'

'We all had a long conversation, just a few hours ago.'

'About the Cosmic Peacemakers,' said Martha. 'And the crystal sphere you gave Captain Carruthers to take to Balmoral.'

'Cosmic who? Never heard of them. And what crystal ball?'

'Arthur, please, you must remember,' begged Carruthers. 'This is urgent – *really* urgent.'

Sir Arthur Conan Doyle said crossly, 'Now listen to me, my boy. The last time we met was for dinner at your parents' house, just over three weeks ago. And I've never seen this charming young lady before in all my life! I am certain

I would remember.' He sighed, and went on: 'Looks to me as if you two have been overdoing it a bit. Spot of lunch in Soho, eh? Bottle of bubbly – or two? Gone to your head!'

'As it happens we did visit the Golden Rose,' said Carruthers stiffly. 'But I assure you, no champagne was drunk. We are both quite sober!'

A hansom cab came by and Conan Doyle hailed it. 'Well, it seems we'll have to agree to differ then. Now, I'm sorry I can't stop, Harry. Important meeting. Going to see the editor of *The Strand Magazine*. He's after more Holmes stories. I'll be at the Grand for a few more days. Pop round and see me and we'll have a nice long chat. Bring your young friend and introduce her to me properly, why don't you?'

He jumped into the cab and it rattled away, leaving Harry Carruthers staring after it with an expression of almost comical astonishment.

He turned to Martha. 'I don't understand it. Arthur's the most honest man I know. What made him lie like that?'

'Maybe that wasn't Arthur Conan Doyle. If these Cosmic Peacemakers really can change their shape, that could have been one of them, just pretending to be Doyle.'

'Nonsense, young lady, nonsense. I know

Arthur Conan Doyle, and that most certainly *was* Arthur Conan Doyle,' insisted Carruthers.

'Yeah, maybe...' said Martha doubtfully. She thought for a moment. 'All right, let's say it is him. I don't think he's lying at all – not as far as he's concerned. He really and truly doesn't remember meeting us. Or giving you that sphere.'

'But how...'

'He's been brainwashed,' said Martha. 'Bits of his memory have been wiped. Remember the way Challoner left the room for a moment, just after you mentioned Doyle's name? The Cosmic Peacemakers are covering their tracks!' She considered. 'Now that *is* something worth telling the Doctor!'

Watched by Carruthers, Martha took a slim metal device from her pocket. She pressed some buttons and held it to her ear. It made a high-pitched whine. She shook it and tried again, still without success.

'No good, I can't reach him.'

'Perhaps he's out of range,' suggested Carruthers. 'Scotland's a long way away.'

She switched the mobile phone off and put it away. 'Believe me, this thing will reach further than that. Besides, I doubt if he's still in Scotland. He'll be chasing Balmoral.'

Carruthers drew a deep breath. 'Now I really could do with a drink! Come on.'

He led the way back into the Grand. They found a quiet table in the lounge under a potted palm. An ancient waiter appeared and Carruthers ordered a bottle of champagne. The waiter staggered off, then returned with surprising speed. He opened the champagne and poured two glasses. Then he put the bottle in a silver ice bucket and moved away.

Carruthers gulped down his champagne, and immediately poured another glass. He looked at Martha, who hadn't touched hers.

'Drink it down. It's good for you. We've been accused of drinking the bubbly, so we might as well do it!'

'Thanks,' Martha told him, 'but I'll stick to water.'

Carruthers shrugged. 'Suit yourself.' He waved to a passing waiter. 'Tonic water for the lady, if you would.' He turned to Martha. 'Unless you'd rather soda?'

'Tonic's fine, thanks.'

'Well,' said Carruthers as Martha's tonic water arrived, 'Doyle can't tell us anything. We can't reach the Doctor, and we discovered very little at the Cosmic Peacemakers. What do we do now?'

'Go back to the Cosmic Peacemakers and find out some more.'

'How? I don't suppose they'll let us in the front door.'

'Then we'll use the back door – if we can find it.' Martha sipped at her tonic water. 'Right,' she said. 'Now, listen carefully. Here's my plan.'

Carruthers listened, becoming more and more shocked as Martha went on. He put down his champagne and did not refill the glass.

'We can't do that!' he said when she'd finished. 'What would the Doctor say?'

Martha shrugged. 'Can't ask him, can we? Anyway, knowing the Doctor, he's probably got enough troubles of his own.'

The Doctor was wading through treacle – at least, that's what it felt like. As soon as he'd got close to the castle, he had come up against an invisible wall. A force field, just as he had expected.

'A very forceful force field,' he muttered. 'Powerful enough to bounce back a charging horseman. But no match for a determined Doctor!'

He took out his sonic screwdriver and took a series of readings. He made some adjustments to the tool, and its end glowed fiercely.

'Aha!' said the Doctor. 'That's sorted it!'

The Doctor made the shape of a big arch with the sonic screwdriver.

'Open Sesame!' he said. He stepped through the arch into the force field – and stuck halfway through.

'Temporary setback,' he muttered.

Swinging his arm with great difficulty he made another arch. He moved a few inches further forward – and stuck again.

Inch by inch the Doctor carved his way through the force field. It was a long and exhausting business. But at long last he popped out the other side. His clothes were a mess and he was panting.

'Judoon technology,' he grumbled. 'Just showing off!'

He ran for the castle.

He reached the walls, apparently unseen. He went through a stone arch and reached a heavy metal-studded door. It creaked open, and the Doctor found himself in a bare stone corridor.

'Tradesman's entrance,' muttered the Doctor. 'Never mind.' He moved carefully forwards. The corridor led to a staircase. The Doctor climbed it and found himself in another corridor. This one was red-carpeted with white and gold pillars along the walls.

'That's more like it! Lords, Ladies and Doctors this way.'

He moved along the corridor, his feet silent on the thick carpeting. Then, suddenly, he heard a steady *thud, thud, thud* coming towards him. He ducked into the alcove behind one of the pillars.

Massive figures appeared at the end of the corridor, six of them marching in strict military formation. Peering from behind the pillar, the Doctor saw gleaming black battle armour, long metal-studded leather tunics, huge boots, belts hung with weapons. And then there were the enormous domed helmets. It was the Judoon, all right, thought the Doctor.

But then, he'd known that all along. Who else stole whole buildings? But what were they up to? That was the question. And who was employing them?

Suddenly the Doctor realised that he wasn't alone in the alcove. Before he could react, a cold circle of steel touched him behind the ear.

A hoarse voice whispered, 'Don't move or I'll kill you! Now, who are you and what are you doing here?'

Chapter Eight

The
Raid

Of all the strange events of a very strange day, thought Captain Harry Carruthers, this was by far the strangest. He was climbing over the rooftops of London's Docklands, with a girl dressed as a boy.

Maybe he should never have ordered the champagne!

As soon as she'd explained her plan, Martha had insisted on returning to his rooms. There she'd made him use his new telephone to contact a number of highly placed officials and civil servants. By making use of his royal connections, Harry had finally reached the right department. Soon afterwards, a messenger had delivered a stack of papers and documents. They were maps and plans of the streets around Black Dog Lane. It hadn't taken Martha long to find what she wanted.

'There!' she said, jabbing her finger at the plan. 'An empty warehouse backing onto the Cosmic Peacemaker laboratories. Just what we need! We'll go in over the roofs.'

Carruthers was horrified. 'My dear girl, don't you realise? I'm a Guards officer. I'm not allowed to carry parcels in the street, let alone commit burglary.'

Martha ignored him. She looked down at her tweed walking outfit, which had been bugging her all day.

'And another thing, I can't go climbing over roofs in this get-up. What kind of clothes have you got here?'

Carruthers was outraged. 'I can assure you that no young ladies are in the habit of keeping their clothes in my rooms!'

Martha laughed. 'I don't mean girls' clothes, you twit, I mean men's clothes. Your clothes will do. You're only a bit taller than me.'

'I hardly think there will be anything suitable.'

'Don't you have any jeans or anything? No, you wouldn't have, would you. What do you wear when you're not dressed up?'

'I'm always dressed up,' said Carruthers simply. 'Hang on a minute...'

He went into his bedroom and opened his

uniform closet. After much searching, he came back with a set of denim overalls.

'I wear these when training. Even Guards officers have to get dirty now and then, and one doesn't want to spoil the bearskin and scarlet tunic.'

'Perfect,' said Martha. She took the overalls from him and went into the bedroom.

A few minutes later, she returned in the denim overalls. The trouser bottoms were rolled up, but they fitted very well. Perhaps a little too well.

'How do I look?'

'Like Vesta Tilley!'

'Who?'

'Music hall performer. She sings dressed as a man.'

'Thanks a lot. They're a bit tight, but they'll do. Now, all I need is an overcoat and hat and I'm all set. Come on!'

With Martha wrapped up in a coat and hat, they'd called a hansom and returned to Black Dog Lane. Martha found the empty warehouse in a nearby alley. She took off her coat and hat and climbed up a drainpipe.

Harry followed. After all, he thought, what else could he do?

Now he was climbing over the warehouse rooftop after Martha, clinging on for dear life.

He found her crouching by a skylight, her form outlined against the sky.

'This is it – I hope! If my calculations are OK, we're directly over the Peacemaker place. Help me get this skylight open.'

Carruthers sighed. In for a penny... 'Move over and let me.'

He leaned over the skylight and knocked out one of the dirty glass panes with his elbow. Glass tinkled down inside. He listened for a moment, but nobody seemed to have heard. He reached inside and slipped the catch. Carefully, he lifted the skylight open.

'You're quite good at this,' whispered Martha. 'If they chuck you out of the Guards, you can start a new career as a gentleman burglar!' She edged past him on the roof. 'I'll go first.'

Before he could stop her, she turned over and slid her legs, then her body, through the open skylight. She hung for a moment at arm's length, then dropped.

Peering through the skylight, Carruthers heard a thud and some very unladylike language. Then Martha's voice floated up.

'Come on! It's not much of a drop.'

Carruthers followed Martha's example. He dropped and landed in a heap on a dusty floor.

Martha helped him to get up.

'There must be a door somewhere...'

Carruthers peered round the dark room. 'Over there,' he said. 'Look, there's a line of light.'

They groped their way across the room, stumbling over all sorts of household objects, including a mangle, a tin bath, an armchair and an old sofa.

Finally, they reached the thin line of light coming faintly under the door. They opened the door quietly and peered out.

It gave onto a grimy corridor which ended in a short steep staircase. Martha and Carruthers crept along the corridor and down the staircase. They found themselves in another world.

They were in a long, curved corridor, its dazzling white walls glowing dimly with soft inner light. There were doors along the wall to either side, and a large set of double doors stood open at the far end. A blaze of light shone out from behind the doors.

'This is more like it,' whispered Martha. She ran her fingers along the wall – it felt smooth and warm to the touch. 'Plastic,' she muttered. 'That hasn't even been invented yet.' She pointed to the double doors. 'Come on. It looks as if the main attraction is down there.'

Moving along the corridor and through the lighted doorway, they found themselves in a huge circular chamber. At its centre was a mass of alien machinery. In a corner of the room was a giant metal archway, which led into shadows.

At the centre of the room was an enormous crystal sphere. There was a fiery vortex at its centre. It hovered over a huge bowl filled with a fiery liquid. A control console stood beside the bowl. Its dials and switches and meters were covered with alien symbols.

Martha and Carruthers moved closer.

'That crystal sphere,' whispered Carruthers. 'It's exactly like the one Doyle gave me to take to Balmoral – only a hundred times bigger. What is this place?'

Vague childhood memories were stirring in Martha's mind. A video she'd been shown in school one rainy afternoon. It had been about the wonders of atomic science.

'I'm not sure,' she said. 'I think it might be a nuclear reactor. Some kind of power source anyway.'

'It is indeed,' said a soft voice behind them. 'Not nuclear but temporal. Power. A force beyond anything your weak human minds can imagine.'

They turned and saw Professor Challoner standing in the glowing archway. He moved into the room.

'Welcome back. It is kind of you to pay me another visit,' said Challoner.

'You don't seem very surprised to see us,' Martha said.

'I knew you would return.'

'Who are you?' said Carruthers angrily. 'What do you want?'

'We are the Peacemakers. Would you like to see our true form?'

Suddenly, the shape of Challoner's face blurred. It grew longer, lizard-like with slanting green eyes, long claws and dripping jaws. He blurred again, and became once more a saintly looking old man.

Martha shuddered. 'I can see why you changed. You didn't say what you wanted.'

'We want your planet.'

'Just you?' demanded Carruthers. 'Or do you have an army hidden away?'

'No, but we have allies.'

He turned as the arch began to blaze more brightly.

A giant figure appeared. It wore black battle armour and a large domed helmet. It held a blaster in its gloved fist.

'I knew it,' whispered Martha. 'Judoon!'

The Judoon trooper marched into the room with a thud of heavy boots.

Then another followed.

'These people are spies,' hissed Challoner. 'They are trespassing and must be punished. Kill them!'

The Judoon raised their blasters and took aim.

A deep voice said, 'Stop!'

A third, even larger Judoon warrior had appeared in the archway.

'It's all right, Captain, we're just executing some rebels,' Challoner said.

'You do not yet have authority over this planet. Therefore they cannot be rebels. Native life forms must not be destroyed without due process.'

'But, I told you, they're spies.'

'There must be a trial.'

'Not guilty!' Martha said, determined to show she wasn't afraid of the Judoon.

Carruthers was still staring at the creatures in wide-eyed astonishment.

'There's no time now,' Challoner sighed. 'Bring them with us. We'll deal with them later.' He moved towards the arch.

The Judoon followed, herding Martha and Carruthers before them.

'Where are you taking us?' demanded Martha.

Challoner turned. 'You should be honoured. You will now see more of the technology of the Cosmic Peacemakers,' he said. 'You're going to Balmoral Castle to see the King!'

He passed through the glowing arch and disappeared.

Martha and Harry and the Judoon followed and disappeared too.

The huge laboratory was empty.

Chapter Nine

The
King

The Doctor reached up and gently pushed the gun away from his ear. 'Don't do that. You'll give me earache.'

'Who are you?' repeated the voice.

'I'm the Doctor, and I've come to help.'

The Doctor turned and found himself facing a thin-faced man in a dark coat. 'And you are?'

'George Fitzroy. I'm one of the King's private secretaries.'

'So what's going on?'

'I only wish I knew.'

'Just tell me what happened.'

The young man sighed. 'I just don't know where to start.'

'Tell you what,' said the Doctor. 'Begin at the beginning. Go on to the end. Then stop. Works for me.'

Fitzroy nodded. 'Well, it started as a perfectly ordinary day. The King had breakfast in bed. He packed poor old Harry Carruthers off to shoot a stag. Then he got up. I was working in my office, looked out and saw it was raining. Except the rain was – this is going to sound so odd – but it was raining *upwards*.'

He rubbed his eyes, still unable to believe what he'd seen. 'Scotland just vanished,' he went on. 'Suddenly there was nothing but sand. Those huge, well, buildings I suppose they are, arrived from the sky and these monsters marched out. You saw one of their patrols just now.'

'Jolly old Judoon,' said the Doctor. 'Go on.'

'There seem to be dozens of them. They've taken over the castle. They rounded everybody up and locked them all in the cellars. They missed me somehow in the rush and confusion. I grabbed a gun and slipped away. I've been dodging them ever since.'

'What about the King?'

'They've got him shut up under guard in the old Queen's sitting room. They seem to be waiting for something.'

'Come on then,' said the Doctor. 'Can't hang round chatting in corridors all day. We'll never save the world like that!'

'Come on where?'

'To see the King.'

'It's too dangerous. We'll be caught.'

'All right. Just show me where the King is, and you can go and hide again. Come on.'

They set off down the corridor.

'I met his mum once, you know, but we didn't really get on,' said the Doctor. 'Wasn't really my fault, to be fair. But Queen Victoria thought I was a bad influence...'

Herded through the Peacemakers' archway, Martha felt an odd sensation. It was as if her entire body was dissolving. The feeling passed, and suddenly she was marching along a wide red-carpeted corridor. It was lined with white pillars and stag-heads hung on the upper walls.

The party stopped outside a set of doors guarded by two Judoon sentries. Professor Challoner pushed them open and they moved inside. The Judoon Captain and the two troopers took up positions around the room.

Martha looked around her. The sitting room they were in was richly furnished. There was a thick red and white checked carpet and two giant sofas, one on each side of a large table in the centre of the room. There were two enormous stuffed armchairs. Everything was covered in a bright tartan. The curtains at the windows were tartan as well. There was a white marble fireplace with a giant mirror over it. Paintings of the Scottish Highlands hung on the walls. It was a cosy, luxurious room, thought Martha. No place for Judoon, or alien lizards disguised as humans.

Seated on one of the armchairs was a very large gentleman with a heavy moustache. He wore a Harris tweed sports jacket and waistcoat, and a kilt. He was smoking an enormous cigar, and he looked calm and rather bored.

Professor Challoner stepped forward and bowed. 'Your Majesty!'

The King glared briefly at the Profressor and then ignored him. His eyes moved lazily over the little group and focused on Carruthers.

'There you are, Harry, my boy. Get your stag this time?'

'Missed again, I'm afraid, Your Majesty.'

The royal gaze turned to Martha. 'Who's your girl friend?' He peered at Martha in her denim overalls. 'It is a girl, isn't it?'

Despite the circumstances, Carruthers smiled. The old boy was on good form.

'Very much so, Your Majesty. Allow me to present Miss Martha Jones. She made me miss my stag.'

'Don't blame you,' said the King promptly.

'Pretty girl like that's worth missing any number of stags.' He gave Martha a gracious royal nod. 'How do you do, my dear.'

Martha felt she couldn't curtsy in overalls, so she bowed.

'I'm good, thank you, Your Majesty. Sorry about the clothes. I didn't know I was coming, and there was no time to change. I've had rather a busy day.'

'Me too, my dear,' said the King. 'Me too!'

Professor Challoner seemed to feel he was being left out of things. 'Forgive me, Your Majesty, but I must insist on your attention. I have come here on a matter of great urgency.'

The King looked bored. 'Still here, are you? Get on with it, then.'

'My name is Professor Challoner. If you will kindly pay close attention, Your Majesty, it will give me great pleasure to explain my Master Plan.'

There was a noise outside the open door and a familiar voice called, 'Out of my way, sentry! Hang on a moment. A Master Plan, eh? Now that's something I've got to hear! I love a good Master Plan. They're such fun.' The Doctor strode confidently into the room.

'Doctor!' cried Martha joyfully.

The Doctor bowed low to the King and gave

the others a friendly nod. 'Your Majesty, Martha, Captain Carruthers.'

'Another friend of yours, Carruthers?' the King asked. 'You do seem to be keeping the strangest company these days.'

'I am sorry, Your Majesty. But I can vouch for the Doctor,' Carruthers said.

'What are you doing here?' Martha asked the Doctor.

'Later,' the Doctor said. 'We mustn't interrupt the Professor. Especially not now I've been vouched for. Carry on, Professor. I do love a good Master Plan. Heard a few Master Plans in my time, mind you. Genghis Khan had a good one, and Napoleon. Well, not that good, perhaps. And the Daleks brought out a new Master Plan every week. Though they never really worked out either, now I come to think of it.'

'Who the devil are you, sir?' Challoner demanded.

'I'm the Doctor. Don't worry about me, just carry on.'

Challoner gave him an angry glare and prepared to speak.

But, before he could get a word out, the Doctor said hopefully, 'Have you got a slide projector? And a pie chart? Nothing like a good pie chart.'

'Be silent, whoever you are,' said Challoner angrily. 'Or I will have you silenced.' He drew a deep breath and started again. 'Your Majesty, you are the ruler of the greatest Empire since the Romans. The Empire upon which the sun never sets.'

'Well aware of that,' grunted the King. 'Think we're ahead of the Romans, actually.' He smoothed his moustache.

'But I can offer you more,' said Challoner dramatically. 'I can make you Emperor of the World!'

Chapter Ten

The Master
Plan

There was a moment of silence.

It was the Doctor who spoke first. As usual, thought Martha, he seemed to have taken centre stage without even trying.

'Bit of a shock for the German Kaiser,' said the Doctor. 'Not to mention the President of France, and the Russian Tsar.'

'Indeed,' agreed the King. He turned to Challoner. 'You're a fool, sir. Germany, France and Russia, all raising armies, all building battleships. If I moved against them, all three countries would combine to crush me – and crush England. What's more, I'm related to most of 'em. Not that that would stop Wilhelm if he thought he could get away with it.'

'Perhaps so, Your Majesty.' said Challoner. 'But suppose you crush them first?'

'And how would I do that?'

'You wouldn't need to, Your Majesty. I will do it for you.'

The King snorted. 'Got an Army and a Navy all ready, have you?'

'They will not be needed, Your Majesty. I shall destroy them by the use of advanced science.'

'Weapons of mass destruction?' suggested the Doctor. 'Spot of atomics? Or is it a neutron bomb? That always goes down well. Goes up first, of course...'

'Nothing so crude,' snarled Challoner. 'We have hidden Temporal Reversion devices in all the major capitals of Europe, Asia and Africa. They can be set off by remote control from the Temporal Power source in my laboratory. The cities, their rulers and their peoples will no longer exist. Your Majesty will be left with an easy conquest.'

'Easy but pointless by the sound of it. What the devil's the fellow talking about?' asked the King.

But the Doctor knew. 'Ooh – that's terribly risky you know. Tricky business, Temporal Reversion. Even the Time Lords left it alone.'

'I am an expert in these matters, Doctor,' said Challoner. 'I can and will do exactly as I promise.' He turned to the King. 'Well, Your Majesty?'

'Don't listen,' burst out Martha. 'You'll just be the puppet emperor of a world under alien rule. He isn't even human!'

'She's right, Your Majesty,' said Carruthers. He turned to the Doctor. 'You know that better than anyone, Doctor. Tell His Majesty.'

The Doctor was silent for a moment. Then he said, 'I don't know. I think it's a pretty neat scheme. Bit risky of course, but well worth a try.'

Martha and Carruthers stared at him in horror.

Challoner too was astonished. He stared at the Doctor. 'Who are you?'

'Just a visitor,' said the Doctor. 'Neutral observer, you might say. Passing through. Sightseeing. Tourist, really. But I think you're onto something. This planet's always been trouble, needs a bit of discipline. You might be just the man – well, not man of course. Monster, alien, whatever.'

Challoner glared at him. 'Your friends do not seem to hold the same opinion.'

'Oh, they're young and impulsive. No sense of the practical. I'll talk them round. Tell you what, give me ten minutes alone with His Majesty and my friends. I'm sure I can convince them.'

'Why should I trust you?'

'What have you got to lose? If I fail, you can always go to Master Plan B. You have got a Plan B, haven't you? You must have a back-up, or do I mean fall-back?'

After a long pause Challoner said, 'Yes, I do have a Plan B, as you put it.'

'Not as good as this one, is it?' said the Doctor. 'The British Empire is best for you, or you wouldn't have started here. Others would be second best.'

'Very well, Doctor, you may have your ten minutes alone.'

'Completely alone, mind you,' said the Doctor. 'No you, and no Judoon.'

'Agreed.' Challoner turned back to the King. 'I advise you to listen to the Doctor, Your Majesty. After all, one puppet is as good as another. As for you, Doctor, permit me to show you who you are dealing with.'

Just as he had in the laboratory, Challoner blurred, and changed back to the lizard-like shape that was his true form.

The Doctor, no stranger to alien life forms, seemed unimpressed. Though he'd seen it before, Carruthers looked on in horror.

Martha turned to the King to see how he was reacting.

Puffing at his cigar, the King said calmly, 'Magic tricks, eh? Damned clever.'

Returning to his human shape, Challoner turned and left the room, followed by the Judoon.

Instantly, Martha and Carruthers rounded on the Doctor.

Martha said, 'Doctor, you can't—'

Carruthers said, 'Sir, I beg of you—'

Both were speaking at once. The Doctor put a finger to his lips, silencing both.

Suddenly the King rose, wheezing a little, and everyone fell silent. He took up a position before the fireplace and stood, a curiously imposing figure, gazing around the room.

'This was my mother's favourite sitting room, you know,' he said, tossing his cigar stub into the fire. 'Never allowed to smoke in here then. Lord, the tickings off I've had in this room!' His gaze fixed on Carruthers. 'You know how long I waited to be King, Harry?'

'A very long time, Your Majesty.'

'All those years as Prince of Wales. She never liked me really. Thought I caused my father's death.'

'I'm sure that's not so, Your Majesty.'

'I got into a bit of a scrape with a young actress. He came down to see me in the country

74

on a wet and windy day, caught a cold and died soon after that. She never forgave me. Said I was thoughtless, never let me take any part in state affairs. Thanks to her long and splendid reign, I was 59 when I came to the throne.' He drew a deep breath. 'So – when I became King, I made up my mind to *be* a King. Heaven knows I've tried. Ain't that so, Harry?'

'Nobody could try harder, Your Majesty.'

The King turned back to the Doctor. 'So you can save your words, Doctor Whoever-you-are. You'd be wasting your breath. I'm not sure who or what this fellow Challoner is, but I want no part of his schemes. My one aim as King is to prevent a world war, not to start one.'

'I'm very glad to hear you say so, Your Majesty,' said the Doctor.

'But you said—' Carruthers began.

'I agree with you both,' said the Doctor quickly. 'Challoner and his mad scheme must be stopped. It's not just mad, it's dangerous. Temporal Reversion Technology is just so unstable. If these devices of his go wrong, and believe me they will, he could warp the fabric of time itself. He could destroy the universe!'

'Then why...' began Martha.

The Doctor cut her off. 'The only way to stop his master plan is to pretend to go along with it. When he comes back, Your Majesty, I want you to agree.'

The King looked unsure. 'And if I don't?'

'He'll carry out Plan B.'

'Which is?'

'He'll kill us,' said the Doctor calmly. 'All of us. Your Majesty included.'

Chapter Eleven

The Honour
of the Judoon

It was obvious to everyone that the Doctor was serious.

'Just a minute,' said Carruthers. 'He seems to be keen on using His Majesty and the British Empire. If he kills him, how will he carry out his plan?'

'No problem,' said the Doctor. 'Master Plan B. He'll kill us all and try to recruit some other crowned head. He'll find one somewhere. Kaiser, Tsar, whoever.'

The King nodded. 'You're right, dammit. Cousin Willy would probably jump at it!'

Martha looked at Carruthers. 'Cousin Willy?'

'The German Kaiser,' he whispered. 'As he said, all the Royals are related.'

'Very well,' said the King. 'For the moment, I'll pretend to agree.'

'Brilliant,' said the Doctor. 'But don't give in

too easily. I want you to demand a few things first...'

When he'd finished talking to the King, the Doctor turned to Martha and Carruthers. 'Now, quickly, there's not much time. Tell me everything you've learned about Challoner.'

'They're calling themselves the Cosmic Peacemakers,' began Martha. 'They've got this hidden lab in Docklands, in a place called Black Dog Lane...'

Challoner returned a few minutes later, with a squad of Judoon at his heels. He found the King standing in the centre of the room, the others grouped behind him.

'I have decided to cooperate with your excellent plan,' said the King grandly. 'The Doctor has convinced me that it is fitting that the British Empire should rule the rest of the world.'

'I am delighted to hear it, Your Majesty.'

'I have two conditions.'

Challoner looked wary. 'Name them.'

'You must return Balmoral Castle to its proper place immediately.'

'It shall be done.'

'The Doctor has agreed to act as my personal agent in this matter. He must be allowed to return to London by his own means and represent me there.'

Challoner seemed doubtful. It was clear that he was still not sure about the Doctor.

'Oh, come on,' said the Doctor. 'You've got the King, the castle, and the Judoon. What harm can I possibly do you on my own? If I go to London, I can smooth the way for you. Do the groundwork. Set things up. Prepare for His Majesty's return, and the boring speeches that will have to follow. He still has to sell your idea to Parliament, you know, if we're going to avoid all those annoying political arguments. Lots of lobbying to be done.'

'Very well,' said Challoner at last.

'Then I'll be off,' said the Doctor. 'Harry, Martha, come along.'

Carruthers shook his head. 'My place is here with the King.'

'Quite right,' said the Doctor. 'Come along then, Martha.'

'No,' said Challoner.

'Oh, play fair. You agreed,' said the Doctor. 'A deal's a deal, even for shape-changing planet-stealers.'

'I agreed only that *you* could leave, Doctor,' Challoner told him. 'Nothing was said about the human female.'

'Miss Jones is my ward, my valued companion. I need her with me.'

'She stays here,' said Challoner. 'And remember, Doctor, your good behaviour guarantees her good health.'

The Doctor gave Martha a worried look.

'Go on, Doctor,' she said. 'I'll stay here and look after Harry.'

The Doctor knew that he had no choice. He needed the TARDIS and his freedom of action.

'Right,' he said. 'Well then, when I'm finished in London, I'll come to Balmoral and pick you up. And remember, Professor Challoner, her good health guarantees your good health.'

Challoner seemed unworried by the threat. 'The Judoon Captain will escort you to the gates, Doctor,' he said.

The Doctor pulled Martha into a hug, shook Carruthers' hand and bowed to the King.

'See you all soon,' he said.

Followed by the Judoon Captain, the Doctor left the room.

At the main door, the Judoon Captain produced and operated a device that opened a path through the force field.

The Doctor looked up at the enormous form beside him.

'I always believed the Judoon were honourable,' he said.

From within the dark helmet above him came a deep, rumbling voice.

'Judoon honour is without flaw or stain.'

'Come off it,' said the Doctor. 'What are you doing mixed up in an act of piracy like this?'

'The Judoon always operate with full legal authority. The path through the force field will close in three Earth minutes.'

The Captain turned and tramped away down the corridor.

'Conversation over,' thought the Doctor. He turned and hurried through the force field.

It took him some time to find the TARDIS – he'd come out of a different exit, and all the dunes looked very much alike.

He found it at last and stood at the top of the dune, looking down at the castle in the desert. He was waiting to see if Challoner would keep his promise.

The blur of the force field faded, the air shimmered and the castle faded away.

Minutes later, the tall spaceships of the Judoon rose slowly into the sky.

The Doctor stood by the TARDIS, lost in thought. He was alone in the vast desert. Except, he remembered, for some very confused desert raiders somewhere in the far distance.

By now the Judoon spaceships, together with Balmoral Castle, should be back in Scotland. The Doctor decided to go and see.

His original plan had been to go to London and deal with the machine that Challoner had built in his laboratory. But Martha was still in Balmoral. If he succeeded at the laboratory, a message might reach Challoner, and Martha would die.

So he could do nothing until Martha was free – which meant going to Balmoral and rescuing her.

Something else was bothering the Doctor – his brief exchange with the Judoon Captain. The Judoon *were* an honourable breed, at least according to their own rather peculiar standards. And they never lied. They saw that as a crime.

Yet the Judoon Captain had insisted that they were acting legally – which was impossible. The only way to find out more was to go to the castle and ask them.

Another good reason to go back to Balmoral.

The Doctor went into the TARDIS. A wheezing, groaning sound disturbed the peace of the Empty Quarter, and then faded away.

The Doctor left the TARDIS, took a moment to get his bearings, then set off for Balmoral Castle. The Highland air was refreshing after the heat of the desert.

He walked on. It didn't take long to get there, and this time the castle was where it was supposed to be.

But, this time, something else was wrong.

The air was full of the crack of rifle fire and the thudding of artillery.

A full-scale pitched battle was raging around Balmoral Castle.

Chapter Twelve

The
Battle

The Doctor climbed a hill overlooking Balmoral Castle and took in the scene.

The entire castle was ringed with troops. Some had dug trenches, others had built walls of sandbags.

Field guns had been set up at various key points. From behind these defences, the soldiers were keeping up heavy and continuous fire.

In the castle grounds stood a number of Judoon. They had not taken shelter, and were returning their attackers' fire with their hand blasters. Occasionally, one staggered under the impact of a rifle bullet, but didn't fall.

A young officer in the advanced trenches outside the castle leaped to his feet. As the Doctor watched, he yelled, 'Come on, chaps. There's only a few of them. Charge!'

The officer dashed forward.

Light streaked from a Judoon blaster and the man exploded in smoke and flame.

Nobody followed him.

Moments later, a lucky shot from a field gun scored a direct hit on one of the Judoon. Its massive body was blown into fragments.

All this had happened in the moments that the Doctor stood watching, horrified. He hated war, always had. 'I've got to stop this,' he muttered, and ran down the hill towards the troops.

As he came closer, a sentry spotted him and raised his rifle.

'Halt!'

Ignoring the rifle, the Doctor ran up to him. 'I need to see your commanding officer, and I need to see him right now!'

The soldier looked doubtfully at him. 'One of his precious scouts are you?'

'Listen to me,' the Doctor said. It was surprising how much he sounded like Harry Carruthers. 'I've got vital information for your commanding officer. Take me to him at once.'

The soldier had been in the Army all his life, and he recognised the snap of authority in the Doctor's voice. 'Command tent's this way, sir.'

He led the Doctor to a small tent, pitched in the shelter of a nearby hill. The soldier went to the open entrance and saluted.

'Gentleman with an important message, General,' the soldier announced. 'Insists on seeing you.'

'Wheel him in!'

The Doctor entered the tent and found a tall, thin uniformed figure with an untidy moustache. He had a map spread out on a table. The General turned to peer at the Doctor. 'You're not one of my fellows.'

'I am the personal envoy of His Majesty,' said the Doctor.

'The King? Where is he?'

'In that castle you're attacking. And a pretty rotten job you're making of it.'

'I'll have you know, young fellow, I know a thing or two about sieges,' said the General. 'Why, when I was in South Africa during the Boer War, I formed a party of scouts. Just lads they were, to carry messages—'

The Doctor cut him off. 'We haven't got time for your memoirs. Just tell me what's been happening here, General. From the beginning, right to the end.'

Just like the sentry, the General found himself responding to the authority in the Doctor's voice.

'We got a message that something was badly wrong at Balmoral. Odd story about the whole place disappearing. When we arrived, the place was here all right – and a group of those big fellows in black were setting up some kind of machinery outside. We challenged them. They ignored us. So we opened fire. Scored a lucky hit on their equipment with a field gun. Then more troops arrived, on both sides, and we settled down for a siege.'

The troops had arrived just as the Judoon were setting up their force field, thought the Doctor. They had destroyed it by a fluke.

'And how's the battle going?'

'Not too well,' admitted the General. 'Rifle bullets don't touch them. You need a direct hit with a field gun, and we don't have enough of them. More on the way, of course, and more troops. But until they get here... They've got some damn nasty weapons. Some kind of heat ray. Who are they anyway – foreign troops?'

'Very foreign,' said the Doctor. His mind was racing. 'Now listen to me General, this siege of yours is madness. You can't hope to defeat them. And if you go on annoying them, they'll bring up more troops. Do you want to see all your men killed?'

The General was stunned. 'So what do you suggest I do?'

'Order a ceasefire and pull back your men.

Let me go and talk to them. I may be able to persuade them to leave peacefully.'

The General looked doubtful. 'You want me to retreat?'

'No, no, no. Well, maybe a tactical retreat if that makes you feel better about it. At least it'll give us time for you to get more troops here.'

'Good thinking,' said the General. 'I'll do it.' He raised his voice and shouted, 'Messenger!'

A soldier ran in and saluted.

The General gave his orders. 'Immediate ceasefire. Pull all the men back.'

The soldier ran from the tent. Minutes later the Doctor heard raised voices.

'Cease fire! General ceasefire! Pull back!'

'Thank you, General,' said the Doctor. 'I'll be off, then. Loads to do and not a lot of time. Oh, and good luck with your Boy Scout movement. I'm sure it'll do very well.'

'How did you know? I've only just started planning it...'

Lieutenant-General Baden-Powell watched in astonishment as the Doctor hurried from the tent.

By the time the Doctor reached the castle, the gunfire had stopped. The soldiers were pulling back. He walked up to the main entrance and found himself facing two Judoon sentries. They covered him with their blasters.

'I'm the Doctor,' he said loudly. 'I was here earlier, remember? I've sent the soldiers away. Now I want to see your Captain. It concerns the honour of the Judoon. So hop to it, go on.'

There was a long pause. Then one of the sentries raised a tube-shaped device and pointed it at the Doctor. There was a series of beeps and a light shone, then the Judoon checked the results of his scan.

'Category: Non-Human,' it announced, before beckoning the Doctor to follow.

The Judoon trooper led the Doctor to a small bare room. Once a storeroom, it had clearly been taken over as a command post.

A massive figure sat with its back to them bending over a complex unit of alien machinery. Some kind of communications device, thought the Doctor.

The sentry spoke in a stream of alien words. Slowly, the Captain turned.

For a moment, the Doctor stared back at the blank, jutting helmet of the Judoon Captain.

Then the Captain reached up and undid the locking clamps, pulling the heavy helmet up and off his head. The Doctor was staring into the face of the Judoon.

It was an impressive sight. The skin on the enormous head was thick and grey and ridged, like that of a rhino. There were two horns, the higher one small, the lower larger, jutting from the centre of the face. The nostrils were flared, and the wide lipless mouth covered rows of yellow teeth that looked like tombstones. Two funny little ears crowned the high, domed forehead.

Most striking of all were the slanting brown eyes. They were strangely intelligent and somehow sad. They stared steadily at the Doctor for a moment.

Curious creatures, the Judoon, thought the Doctor. Brutal and savage, yet not without morals of their own. Now everything depended on how well he had judged them.

Waving the sentry away, the Captain touched the translation device on his breastplate.

'Earth English,' the deep voice boomed. 'Why have you returned, Doctor? The Peacemakers have decided you are an enemy. They demand your execution.' The Judoon Captain drew his blaster and pointed it straight at the Doctor. 'Do you wish to die?'

Chapter Thirteen

Revenge

The Doctor ignored the threat. 'At the gate, when I left, you said the Judoon were here under full legal authority. That cannot be true.'

'You say that I lie?' rumbled the deep voice.

'No. I think someone has lied to you. Take it from me, this invasion cannot be legal.'

'The operation has been authorised by the Galactic Council.'

'That's impossible. Such an action is against Galactic Diplomatic Policy.'

The Judoon Captain produced a scroll. 'This scroll bears the seal of the Council. It states that Earth is a hopelessly warlike planet. It has been handed over to the Cosmic Peacemakers. My Judoon are fully authorised to assist in this process.'

'May I?' The Doctor took the document and studied the massive seal.

'The seal is genuine.'

'Oh yes, the seal is genuine,' said the Doctor. 'You're right there. Proper authentic seal, that. This seal is so genuine that it's got flippers and eats fish. But the scroll... Well that's as genuine as a nine bob note. Or a 45p piece. Take your pick.'

He took out his sonic screwdriver and adjusted it, then used it to shine a violet light over the scroll. The lettering on the scroll faded, allowing other lettering to show through beneath.

'Your Peacemaker friends took a genuine Council scroll and altered its meaning. You see the changes here... and here and here... If I just resonate it a little, you can see what the document really says.' Letters faded away and were replaced by others. The Doctor turned off his sonic screwdriver and let the scroll roll back up with a snap. He held it out. 'Here you go.'

The Judoon Captain took the scroll and unrolled it again. He studied it carefully, reading out loud in his deep rumbling voice.

'Earth must be left alone to work out its own destiny.' The Captain threw down the scroll with a cry of distress. 'We have been betrayed. Judoon honour is stained.' He turned his massive face towards the Doctor. 'Tell me – what must we do?'

'Leave,' said the Doctor promptly. 'Clear out immediately before you do any more harm. I have friends on the Galactic Council. I'll see that they learn the truth. You'll get off with slapped wrists. Probably ban you from getting involved in Earth's affairs from now on. Satellites and colonies only, that sort of thing.'

The Judoon Captain drew in a deep breath, then nodded slowly. He spoke into his communication device. 'Evacuate! All units evacuate immediately.'

One thing you could say for the Judoon, thought the Doctor, they knew how to obey orders. Almost before the Captain's voice had died away, the castle corridors were echoing with the tramp of departing Judoon.

The Judoon Captain rose, tucking his helmet under his arm. 'We leave now, Doctor. But I have one final task. My honour has been stained. I must have revenge.' Before the Doctor could reply, he stamped off.

Fearing the worst, the Doctor hurried after the Judoon Captain. The huge creature marched down the castle corridors, cutting through the squads of Judoon going the other way.

They reached the Queen's Sitting Room and found Professor Challoner standing in the doorway. Behind him, three of the white-robed

Peacemakers were holding Martha, Carruthers and the King at blaster-point.

Martha and Carruthers were poised and tense, ready for any chance to escape. Back in his armchair, the King had just lit another cigar.

As the Judoon Captain strode into the room, one of the Peacemakers shrieked at him. 'What's happening? Why are your troops leaving?'

'You lied,' roared the Captain.

The Peacemaker turned his blaster on the Judoon. But the Captain drew his blaster with blinding speed.

The Doctor skidded into the room behind the Judoon Captain.

'Wait!' he shouted as he saw what the Captain was about to do. 'You can arrest them. There's no need to—'

But the Captain ignored the Doctor, and fired. The Peacemaker burst into flame under the impact of the blaster ray. Changing back for a moment into his lizard-like shape, he crumbled into fiery ashes.

The Captain fired again and again, and the other two Peacemakers exploded in flames.

The Captain swung round to face Challoner. 'And now you, their leader.'

'No!' screamed Challoner. 'I'm your friend. We can rule this world together—'

'You lied,' said the Captain and raised his blaster. 'You have stained the honour of the Judoon. Verdict: guilty. Penalty: death. Execute.' The Judoon Captain prepared to fire.

'This isn't the way!' the Doctor yelled. He ran to stop the Captain, but the Judoon swept him aside.

While the Judoon Captain was distracted, Challoner leaped behind Martha. He wound an arm around her neck and held her before him as a shield.

'Don't shoot!' shouted the Doctor, as the Judoon Captain moved towards Challoner.

'I can conquer this world without your help, you stupid brute,' shrieked Challoner. 'You'll see, you'll see!'

He produced a compact but complex device from beneath his robe and touched a control. There was a flash of purple light, and he and Martha vanished together.

'He has escaped,' growled the Captain. 'Revenge is incomplete.'

The Doctor looked at the three heaps of ash on the floor. 'You didn't do too badly.' He shook his head and sighed. 'Be happy with that. I'll deal with Challoner for you. In my own way.'

The Judoon Captain studied him for a moment. 'I trust to your honour, Doctor.

Destroy him and restore mine. In return, I give my word of honour that no Judoon will set foot on this planet again.' He turned and marched from the room.

'Doctor, what about Martha?' said Harry Carruthers. 'We must find her.'

'I know where he's taken her,' said the Doctor. 'Don't worry, I'll deal with him. You look after the King!'

As the Doctor ran from the room, the King spoke for the first time. 'Odd fellow, that friend of yours, Harry. Never still for a moment!'

The Doctor sprinted for the TARDIS, ignoring shouts from a group of soldiers nearby. As he reached the door, he heard a roaring in the sky. He turned and looked back. Three huge spaceships were rising into the sky.

True to their word, the Judoon were leaving.

Chapter Fourteen

Blowback

Inside the TARDIS, the Doctor was studying the screen again. This time it showed a map of London's Docklands – Black Horse Lane.

The Doctor's hand moved rapidly over controls and a pulse of light appeared on the screen. 'There we are!' muttered the Doctor. 'A Temporal Reversal Generator, if ever I saw one. Wonder where he nicked that from. Far too advanced for Challoner.' He moved quickly round the TARDIS console, adjusting controls and checking readouts. 'If I lock onto the pulse... Tricky, mind you, very tricky.' The Doctor paused and grinned. 'Just as well I'm a genius...'

His fingers flashed over the controls.

In his laboratory, Challoner too was busy, working at the console beside the giant crystal sphere. The sphere itself pulsed with light, growing steadily brighter.

The pool of liquid in the bowl below bubbled and seethed.

Close beside him, propped against the wall, Martha looked on helplessly.

The instant they'd arrived, Challoner had gripped her neck with long bony fingers. He tightened his grip until Martha was half-conscious. Then he took a roll of plastic tape from a drawer and bound her wrists and ankles. By the time she was fully conscious again, she was tied so firmly that she couldn't move.

She wondered why Challoner hadn't killed her. Perhaps he needed an audience. Or perhaps he was afraid the Doctor might find them.

'The power is building up nicely,' Challoner said. 'When it is at its peak, I will trigger the Temporal Remote Control devices. Paris, Berlin, Tokyo, Moscow, all the major cities of the world will cease to exist.'

'What good will that do you? The Judoon have gone, and the Doc—'

'I shall recruit other soldiers – warriors from Schlangi, or Ogrons perhaps. When I am ruler, I shall hunt down the Doctor and kill him.' He paused. 'No, I shall kill you in front of him,' Challoner decided. 'And then I shall kill him.'

Martha decided the shock of defeat had turned his brain. 'You needn't worry about finding the Doctor,' she said bravely. 'I'd worry about him finding you.'

As if to prove her words, the TARDIS materialised, and the Doctor stepped out. He looked at the pulsing crystal sphere.

'Spot on! Now, that's pretty impressive steering if I say so myself – and I do say so. Do you say so?' He looked at Martha. 'Brilliant stuff! Oh – a bit tied up, are we?' He turned to Challoner. 'Now I think it's time you switched that piece of junk off before it all goes horribly wrong.'

'Do you really think so, Doctor?'

'I know so.'

'You're wrong,' said Challoner. 'The power has almost built up, and in a few moments I shall trigger the remote controls.'

'Not if it overloads.'

'And what's going to make it overload, Doctor?' asked Challoner. He picked up an alien blaster gun and waved it at the Doctor.

'I am!' said the Doctor.

Martha realised that the Doctor had his sonic screwdriver in his hand. He pointed it at the console, and its tip glowed with a blue light.

The console burst into smoke and flame. The giant crystal sphere began to pulse violently.

With a scream of rage, Challoner aimed his blaster at the Doctor.

Although her wrists and ankles were tied, Martha was only a few feet from Challoner. She braced herself against the wall, then launched herself at him, hitting Challoner with her whole body.

Challoner staggered back. The edge of the bowl under the enormous sphere caught him behind the knees. He tumbled over it, falling into the bubbling liquid.

The Doctor peered into the bowl. He caught a glimpse of a wriggling lizard-like shape. Then it faded away.

'Look out!' screamed Martha, gazing upwards.

The crystal sphere glowed fiercely. Then it exploded, showering fragments of crystal down into the laboratory.

The Doctor grabbed Martha and dragged her clear. He fished an ancient penknife from his pocket, cut her bonds and helped her up.

'I said it would all go wrong,' he told her.

Martha peeled the rest of the tape from her wrists and ankles. She looked at the wrecked machinery. 'Is that stuff safe now?'

Before the Doctor could answer, the console glowed briefly. Then the console, the pool and the crystal fragments simply disappeared.

'What happened?'

'Temporal blowback,' said the Doctor. 'It's abolished itself. Not only doesn't it exist now, but it never did.'

'And Challoner?'

'Him too. Now come on Martha, looks like we've got a very busy schedule ahead of us!'

Martha was outraged. 'What? I thought it was all over. I was looking forward to a bit of that gracious living you promised me.'

'You can have it,' said the Doctor. 'Just not in London.'

'Where then?'

'Everywhere!'

'What are you on about?'

The Doctor waved an arm around the wrecked laboratory.

'This may be harmless now. But what about all the Temporal Reversion Devices it was meant to trigger? We don't want humans getting crude time engineering too early. And suppose they start going off on their own. No, we need to track them all down.'

'I see.'

'Fancy a lightning tour of the world's capitals, Martha? Paris, Rome, Berlin, Tokyo, Moscow, Beijing...'

He opened the TARDIS door.

'Now let's get this clear, Doctor. You're offering me a top-speed, if-it's-Wednesday-it-must-be-China tour of the world. With, as an added attraction, an unstable alien device to be discovered and defused in each city?'

'Well, you could put it like that... But five star. Definitely five star.'

'A sort of bomb-disposal team's working holiday?'

'In a way...'

Martha didn't answer. She turned away so the Doctor couldn't see her smile, and strode into the TARDIS.

The Doctor followed her. 'Come on, Martha, you'll love Beijing. And as for Moscow...'

The door closed behind them.

The TARDIS wheezed and groaned and went on its way.

Quick Reads

Books in the Quick Reads series

www.quickreads.org.uk

Quick Reads

Pick up a book today

Quick Reads are bite-sized books by bestselling writers and well-known personalities for people who want a short, fast-paced read. They are designed to be read and enjoyed by avid readers and by people who never had or who have lost the reading habit.

Quick Reads are published alongside and in partnership with BBC RaW.

We would like to thank all our partners in the Quick Reads project for their help and support:

The Department for Innovation, Universities and Skills
NIACE
unionlearn
National Book Tokens
The Vital Link
The Reading Agency
National Literacy Trust
Welsh Books Council
Basic Skills Cymru, Welsh Assembly Government
Wales Accent Press
Lifelong Learning Scotland
DELNI
NALA

Quick Reads would also like to thank the Department for Innovation, Universities and Skills; Arts Council England and World Book Day for their sponsorship and NIACE for their outreach work.

Quick Reads is a World Book Day initiative.
www.quickreads.org.uk   www.worldbookday.com

Other resources

Free courses are available for anyone who wants to develop their skills. You can attend the courses in your local area. If you'd like to find out more, phone 0800 66 0800.

 Don't get by get on 0800 66 0800

A list of books for new readers can be found on www.firstchoicebooks.org.uk or at your local library.

 The Vital Link

Publishers Barrington Stoke (www.barringtonstoke.co.uk), New Island (www.newisland.ie) and Sandstone Press (www.sandstonepress.com) also provide books for new readers.

The BBC runs a reading and writing campaign. See www.bbc.co.uk/raw.

2008 is a National Year of Reading. To find out more, search online, see www.dius.gov.uk or visit your local library.

www.quickreads.org.uk   www.worldbookday.com

Quick Reads

Doctor Who: I Am a Dalek
by Gareth Roberts

BBC Books

Equipped with space suits, golf clubs and a flag, the Doctor and Rose are planning to live it up on the Moon, Apollo-mission style. But the TARDIS has other plans, landing them instead in a village on the south coast of England; a picture-postcard sort of place where nothing much happens...until now.

Archaeologists have dug up a Roman mosaic, dating from the year 70 AD. It shows scenes from ancient myths, bunches of grapes – and a Dalek. A few days later a young woman, rushing to get to work, is knocked over and killed by a bus. Then she comes back to life.

It's not long before all hell breaks loose, and the Doctor and Rose must use all their courage and cunning against an alien enemy – and a not-quite-alien accomplice – who are intent on destroying humanity.

Featuring the Doctor and Rose as played by David Tennant and Billie Piper in the hit series from BBC Television.

Quick Reads

Doctor Who: Made of Steel
by Terrance Dicks

BBC Books

A deadly night attack on an army base. Vehicles are destroyed, soldiers killed. The attackers vanish as swiftly as they came, taking highly advanced equipment with them.

Metal figures attack a shopping mall. But why do they only want a new games console from an ordinary electronics shop? An obscure government ministry is blown up – but, in the wreckage, no trace is found of the secret, state-of-the-art decoding equipment.

When the TARDIS returns the Doctor and Martha to Earth from a distant galaxy, they try to piece together the mystery. But someone – or something – is waiting for them. An old enemy stalks the night, men no longer made of flesh...

Featuring the Doctor and Martha as played by David Tennant and Freema Agyeman in the hit series from BBC Television.